j
PB
ENDERLE

Dear Timothy Tibbitts

Dear Timothy Tibbitts

by *Judith Ross Enderle* and
Stephanie Gordon Tessler

illustrated by Carolyn Ewing

MARSHALL CAVENDISH   NEW YORK

Dear Cheryl,
    We're so glad you're our best friend. All the letters in this book are for you. Please write us back soon.

            Love,
            Stephanie and Judy

    For Lisa, Vanessa, and Mark
                — C. E.

Text copyright © 1997 by Judith Ross Enderle and Stephanie Gordon Tessler
Illustrations © 1997 by Carolyn Ewing
All rights reserved
Marshall Cavendish, 99 White Plains Road, Tarrytown, New York 10591
The text of this book is set in 15 point Usherwood Medium
The illustrations are rendered in watercolors
First Edition
Printed in Italy

Library of Congress Cataloging-in-Publication Data
Enderle, Judith R.
Dear Timothy Tibbitts / by Judith Ross Enderle and Stephanie Gordon Tessler ; illustrated by Carolyn Ewing.
p.   cm. Summary: Envious of the many letters his father, mother, and visiting cousin get in the mail,
six-year-old Timothy writes a pretend letter to a friend and gets a surprise back.
ISBN 0-7614-5009-2
[1. Letters—Fiction. 2. Cousins—Fiction.] I. Tessler, Stephanie Gordon. II. Ewing, C. S., ill. III. Title.
PZ7.E6965De   1997   [E]—dc21   96-47369 CIP AC

1 3 5 7 8 6 4 2

Every day, except Sunday, Mr. Sloan's mail cart clickety-clacks over the sidewalk cracks. "Here, boy. Come get a treat," he calls to Dooley, the dog who lives next door to my friend Marcus.

I rush to meet Mr. Sloan. When he hands me the mail I
ask, "Are there any letters for me?"
And every day, except Sunday, he says, "No letter for Mr.
Timothy Tibbitts today. Maybe tomorrow."

As I run back to the house, I pass the garden where my mom is weeding the beans. "Jillions of letters for you," I tell her. "But I never get even one letter."

"Maybe tomorrow," she says, and waves her trowel at me.

Inside, my dad calls from the kitchen. The lemons he's squishing have a sharp, summertime smell. My dad makes the best lemonade in the whole wide world.

"One dillion letters for you today," I say, and plop down on a chair. "But there isn't even one for me."

"Maybe tomorrow," he says. He sips some lemonade, then makes a sour face.

"Is the mail here?" asks my cousin Emma Kay, skipping into the kitchen. Emma Kay is ten and wears earrings. And she's staying with us all summer. She sleeps on the couch in the den.

"There are at least a gazillion letters for you, Emma Kay," I say. "Of course there isn't even one letter for me."

"Of course," says Emma Kay. She tears open her first letter. "This is from my very best friend, Margo."

I follow her to the front porch. "Maybe tomorrow I'll get a letter."
"No, you won't get a letter," she says, sitting on the step to read.
"Why not?" I ask.
Emma Kay gives me a "be quiet" look. "Timothy, I'm busy reading my letter," she says.

And after lunch, Emma Kay is too busy writing to talk.
"Can I please write a letter?" I ask. I pick up a pencil.
Emma Kay gives me paper with blue lines. "Now shush,"
she says.
I don't talk. I just write.

"Can I please have an envelope?" I ask.
Emma Kay hands me one. Then she licks a stamp and sticks it on her envelope.
I fold up my letter and put it in my envelope.
"Can I please have a stamp?" I ask.

"No, Timothy. Stamps are for real letters," says Emma Kay.
"This is a real letter," I tell her.
I draw my own stamp on my envelope.

The next day...clickety-clack. Clickety-clack. I hear the mail cart coming.

"Here, Dooley," calls Mr. Sloan. He gives Dooley a treat. My house is next. "Sorry. There's no letter for Mr. Timothy Tibbitts today," says Mr. Sloan.

"That's okay," I say. "Today I'm mailing a letter."

"Well now," says Mr. Sloan. "That's a fine-looking letter."

"It's for my friend Marcus," I say.

"So it is,"says Mr. Sloan as he puts my letter in his cart.

Then he hands me a pile of mail. There are letters for my
mom. There are letters for my dad. And there are more
letters for my cousin Emma Kay.

The next day is Saturday. "Come and play," Marcus calls
from his yard.
"I can't," I call back. "I have to go to the movies with Emma
Kay," I say.
"Have fun!" says Marcus. He runs back to Dooley's house to play.
I wonder if he got my letter yet.
Before I can ask him, Emma Kay says it's time to go.

"I like to go to the movies," I tell Emma Kay as we get on the bus. "But I would rather wait for Mr. Sloan."

"That's silly," says Emma Kay. "Movies are so-oo much better than letters."

"I don't think so-oo," I tell her. Sometimes I wish she'd go home.

When we come home, there are a bagillion letters in the mailbox, but not even one letter for me. Maybe Marcus was too busy playing with Dooley to write back.

Clickety-clack. Clickety-clack. On Monday I run to the mailbox. "Timothy Tibbitts, you're late today," calls Mr. Sloan. Our mailbox is full of letters. I take them out and hurry into the house.

Mom and Dad and Emma Kay are having lemonade and cookies. One glass of lemonade is still full. One oatmeal cookie has no bites missing.

"There are jillions of letters for Mom," I say. "And dillions of letters for Dad."

"Did I get any letters?" Emma Kay asks.

"Gazillions," I say. "And I got a letter today."

"Wonderful!" says my mom.

"Let's see it," says my dad.

"Who sent it?" asks Emma Kay.

I hold up the letter.
"It says Timothy Tibbitts on it. It's from Marcus."
"How do you know it's from Marcus?" asks Emma Kay.
"Because I wrote a letter to him."
My letter has a real stamp and neat printing.
I open the letter.

Timothy Tibbitts
403 West 24th St.
Newton, Ks. 641

"Thank you, Emma Kay," I say.

"You're welcome," says Emma Kay.

"Excuse me please," I say.

"Where are you going?" asks Emma Kay.

"To write a letter," I say.

HOW TO WRITE A FRIENDLY LETTER

Date

DEAR and your friend's NAME goes here,

Tell your friend why you are writing. Write the same way that you talk. You might share things you've been doing or something interesting you've seen. Maybe you've just read a good book you want to share.

It's okay to ask your friend to write back.

BEST or LOVE goes here,

Sign your name

Your name
Your street address
Your city, state, and zip code

Your friend's name
Your friend's street address
Your friend's city, state, zip code

ON THE ENVELOPE